# This is Ella

by **Krista Ewert**

Illustrated by **Celia Marie Baker**

 FriesenPress

Suite 300 – 990 Fort St
Victoria, BC, V8V 3K2
Canada

www.friesenpress.com

ISBN
978-1-5255-1360-2 (Hardcover)
978-1-5255-1361-9 (Paperback)
978-1-5255-1362-6 (eBook)

1. JUVENILE FICTION, SOCIAL ISSUES, SPECIAL NEEDS

Distributed to the trade by The Ingram Book Company

To my beautiful Ella

This is Ella.

Ella is seven years old and likes to go to school.
Every day she packs her lunch and puts on
her backpack.

*Do you go to school too?*

Ella has blond hair and blue eyes.
She wears pink glasses.

Do you have blue eyes too?
Or do you have brown eyes?
Maybe your eyes are green.
Or purple.
Or maybe even aquamarine.

Ella is small. She might be smaller than you
and she might not run as fast as you

8

but she still wants to be included...

*just like you.*

Ella can count to ten and knows all of her letters.
She can set the table and help her baby sister
get a drink of milk.

*What do you help with at home?*

Ella loves to dance and ride her bike.
Ella's bike is blue with a basket on the front.

*Do you have a bike?*
*What colour is it?*

Ella has Down syndrome.

Down syndrome is not a disease. You cannot catch Down syndrome; it is something that Ella was born with.

Ella wants to be treated with respect. Sometimes Ella needs help and sometimes she likes to do things by herself...

*just like you.*

Ella has a hard time saying some words.
She has to practice some words just like
she has to practice sitting still.

*Do you have to practice sitting still?*
*What are other things you have to practice?*

Ella can be a good friend.

She can play games and run and jump
and climb.

She can laugh and share and sometimes she can
be very, very silly.

*Do you like to be silly?*

Ella likes to learn and play but most of all,
Ella loves to be with her friends.

*What do you think it means*
*to be a good friend?*

# Acknowledgements:

Thank you to God, our Father, who in His infinite grace and mercy gave us Ella.

Thank you to everyone on TEAM ELLA; you know who you are. I would especially like to thank our kindergarten team captains, Janesse Boudreau and Carolyn Morgan-Chan, who gave us such an empowering start to Ella's school journey—this book would not exist without you. Thank you to Janesse for helping this become a valuable teaching tool. Thank you to Celia Baker for so perfectly depicting Ella in illustrated form. Thank you to Ben, my best friend, father of my children, and the hand that pulls me up from the mire every time I fall. Thank you to my kids: Jakob, Ella, and Audrey, who teach me God's love, joy, and patience every single day. Thank you to my mom, Joy, who lives by her name and has always been my biggest fan and cheerleader. Thank you to Dad, Karin, Ryan, and the rest of my family for loving Ella so deeply. Finally, thank you to all of you, near and far, who have journeyed with us through these turbulent years. I am grateful.

# About Down syndrome

Down syndrome, also known as Trisomy 21, is a genetic variation, which results in individuals having an extra copy of the twenty-first chromosome for a total of 47 chromosomes, instead of the typical 46. This can be diagnosed through a simple blood test. Essentially, having Trisomy 21 means there is extra of the genetic material contained in that chromosome. Think about it this way: do you like smoothies? I like to make mine with banana, yogurt, orange juice, and maybe some strawberries. Yummm! Now, what would happen if you added double the amount of strawberries? Your smoothie is going to look redder and taste a little bit different.

In people with Down syndrome, the "extra" manifests itself in different ways. Often these individuals tend to have a flattened nose bridge, almond-shaped eyes that are upward-slanting, low muscle tone, and small hands and feet. Sometimes, their hearts have trouble working on their own or they might have trouble eating. It also often results in developmental delays in speech, cognition, learning, and/or physical development.

Fifty years ago, people with Down syndrome would not have been expected to live very long and would be separated from the rest of society. Most people thought that they couldn't help them, but that was not true. Today, once we know that a baby has Down syndrome, we can start helping him or her right away. It makes a big difference. People check their hearts to make sure they are working properly; if not, they get them fixed right away. Other people help them learn how to speak, eat, walk, and do any of the other things that they have trouble learning on their own.

Every day we are learning more and more about Down syndrome. We now know that individuals who are born with Down syndrome can do most of the things that people without the extra chromosome can do. They can play, dance, and learn. They can have jobs, live on their own, and contribute to communities in very meaningful ways...*just like you.*

To obtain a copy of the accompanying lesson plan please visit:
www.kristaewert.com/this-is-ella-book

CPSIA information can be obtained
at www.ICGtesting.com
Printed in the USA
LVHW071642030820
662265LV00026B/528